Healthy Snacks with Blue!

by J-P Chanda • illustrated by Dan Kanemoto

Simon Spotlight/Nick Jr.
New York London Toronto Sydney

Based on the TV series *Blue's Clues*® created by Traci Paige Johnson, Todd Kessler, and Angela C. Santomero as seen on Nick Jr.® On *Blue's Clues*, Joe is played by Donovan Patton. Photos by Joan Marcus.

SIMON SPOTLIGHT
An imprint of Simon & Schuster Children's Publishing Division
1230 Avenue of the Americas, New York, New York 10020

Manufactured in the United States of America
10 9 8 7 6 5 4 3
ISBN-13: 978-1-4169-2778-5
ISBN-10: 1-4169-2778-6

One day at school, Miss Marigold had a special assignment.

"Tomorrow we are going to have our very first Healthy Snack Day, so I want each of you to bring your favorite healthy snack for the class to share."

"Yummy!" said Magenta. "I know just what to bring."

"Me too!" said Purple Kangaroo.

It seemed like everyone knew the special snack they wanted to share—everyone except Blue.

Blue wanted her snack to be really special. She wanted to bring the best, healthiest snack of all. The trouble was, she liked so many!

"There are fruits and vegetables and nuts and grains. . . ."

"Wow, Blue. There really are a lot of healthy snacks," said Joe.

"And they're all so yummy," said Blue.

“So how will you decide which one to bring to class?” asked Joe.

Blue knew exactly who to ask for help in deciding what to bring.

Mr. Salt and Mrs. Pepper were ready to help!

"What a terrific assignment!" said Mr. Salt. "Think of all the different kinds of healthy treats you can pick."

"Which kind do you like the best?" asked Mrs. Pepper.

Blue scratched her head. She wanted to bring a treat that was sweet and juicy and fun to eat. . . .

"I know!" she said. "I will bring fruit!"

"Great choice, Blue!" cheered Joe. "But what kind of fruit?"

Blue had a great idea. "We can make a big fruit salad with all different kinds of fruits!" said Blue.

"What a terrific idea!" Mrs. Pepper said.

"It's time for a field trip!" said Mr. Salt.

Mr. Salt and Mrs. Pepper took Blue and Joe to the market to gather the ingredients for Blue's fruit salad. There was so much delicious fruit to choose from!

"How about something crunchy," Joe suggested.

"Like apples," said Blue.

"Maybe something with a fun color," Mr. Salt said.

"Like oranges," said Blue.

"Or *blue*berries," said Joe. He and Blue giggled.

Some fruits were very big.

"How about a cantaloupe? Or watermelon?" asked Mrs. Pepper.

Some were much smaller.

"Raspberries? Grapes?" asked Mr. Salt.

"There are so many different kinds of fruits to choose from!" said Blue.

"I think I need one more thing to make my fruit salad really special," said Blue.

"What about raisins?" said Joe.

Blue thought for a moment. She'd never tasted raisins before.

"Oh, I don't know if I like raisins," Blue said.

"You won't know until you try," said Mrs. Pepper.

Blue agreed and tasted one. “Hey! These are good.”

Blue added raisins to their shopping cart, which was full. She had everything she needed for her fruit salad. It was time to head home.

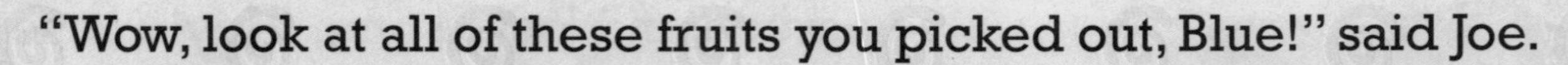
"Wow, look at all of these fruits you picked out, Blue!" said Joe.

"And every one of them is healthy," said Mrs. Pepper.

"And perfect for your fruit salad!" said Mr. Salt.

RAISINS

"Now, where do we start?" asked Blue.

"With chef's hats, of course," said Mr. Salt.

Joe and Blue put on their hats, washed their hands, and got to work.

RAISINS

Mr. Salt and Mrs. Pepper helped Blue and Joe prepare the fruit salad.

They washed all of the fruits and patted them dry.

Mr. Salt chopped the apples. Mrs. Pepper peeled the oranges.

Joe and Blue scooped out the melon into balls.

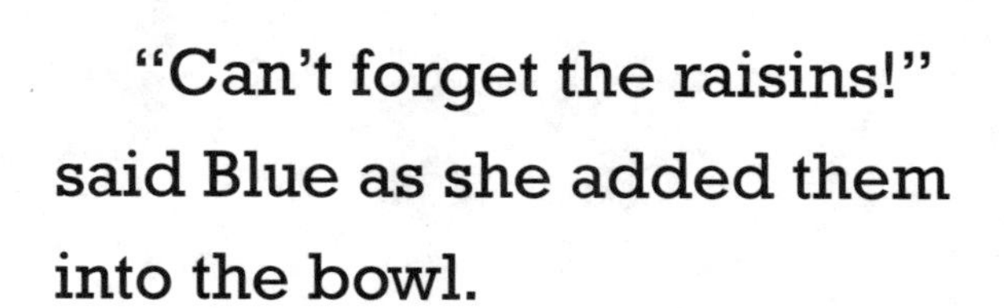

"Can't forget the raisins!" said Blue as she added them into the bowl.

Blue couldn't wait for her friends to try her healthy snack.

At school everyone was very excited about Healthy Snack Day. Miss Marigold set all of the snacks out on a table so the whole class could have a taste.

Magenta brought in crunchy carrots.

Green Puppy brought celery sticks that snapped with each bite.

Purple Kangaroo had three kinds of nuts in a bowl.

Periwinkle made a salad with lettuce, tomatoes, and cucumbers.

"What terrific snacks you've all brought in," said Miss Marigold.

Blue was having fun trying each of the snacks. Her fruit salad was next!

Would they like it? Would it taste as good as all of the other treats?

Magenta took a bite, then Periwinkle, then Purple Kangaroo.

One by one, everyone in the class had a taste of Blue's fruit salad. She watched and waited and wondered what they thought. . . .

"Mmmmmm," said Periwinkle.

"This is so yummy, Blue!" cheered Magenta.

Everyone loved it!

"I think Healthy Snack Day was a big success," said Miss Marigold.

"We should eat healthy snacks every day!" said Blue.

All of her friends agreed. It was a perfectly healthy idea!